MARY HOFFMAN has written more than 70 books for children and in 1998 was made an Honorary Fellow of the Library Association for service to children and libraries. She is also the editor of a quarterly children's book review called Armadillo. Her book *Song of the Earth* (Orion) was shortlisted for the Kurt Maschler Award in 1995 and won the Primary English Award for that year. In 1992 *Amazing Grace*, her first book for Frances Lincoln, was selected for Child Education's Best Books of 1991 and Children's Books of the Year 1992, commended for the Kate Greenaway Medal and included on the National Curriculum Reading List in 1996 and 1997. Its sequel, *Grace & Family*, was among Junior Education's Best Books of 1995 and was shortlisted for the Sheffield Libraries Book Award 1996. It was followed by *An Angel Just Like Me*, *A Twist in the Tail*, *Three Wise Women*, *Women of Camelot*, *Seven Wonders of the Ancient World* and a Grace story-book, *Starring Grace*. She has collaborated with Jackie Morris on *Parables: Stories Jesus Told*, *Miracles: Wonders Jesus Worked* and *Animals of the Bible*.

KARIN LITTLEWOOD was born and brought up in Yorkshire. She took her B.A. in graphic design at Newcastle Polytechnic and M.A. in illustration at Manchester Polytechnic. Since 1999 she has specialised in illustrating children's books, among them *The Lonely Whale*, written by David Bennett (David Bennett Books), *Sun Slices, Moon Slices* by Adèle Geras (Scholastic), *Say a Little Prayer* by Burt Bacharach (The Chicken House) *Billy's Sunflower* by Nicola Moon (Scholastic) and *Chanda and the Mirror of Moonlight* by Margaret Bateson Hill (published in English and Hindustani by Zero to Ten). — received a Kate Greenaway nomination in 2001 for *Swallow Journey* by Vivian French (Zero to Ten) and was shortlisted for the Federation of Children's Books Award 2001 for *Ellie and the Butterfly Kitten* (Orchard).

For Suleiman, Josè, Naima, Dagma, Flavia, Brunilda, Hagar,
Jo, Hasna and all the others who had to leave their first homes
and were brave enough to find new ones – M.H.

For Christina – K.L.

ARABIC WORDS

qu'ran (**Koran**)
The sacred book of Islam, believed by Moslems
to be the word of God revealed to Mohammed

hajab
Traditional head covering worn
by Moslem women

The Colour of Home copyright © Frances Lincoln Limited 2002
Text copyright © Mary Hoffman 2002
Illustrations copyright © Karin Littlewood 2002

First published in Great Britain in 2002 by
Frances Lincoln Limited, 4 Torriano Mews
Torriano Avenue, London NW5 2RZ

www.franceslincoln.com

With thanks for help to Jill Rutter, formerly of the Refugee Council, Sandi Santos, formerly
of Homeless Action in Barnet, Sahra Haid at the Tawakal Somali Women's Group in Limehouse
and Laila Jama at the Haringey Somali Community Association

British Library Cataloguing in Publication Data available on request

ISBN 0-7112-1991-5 paperback

Set in Cochin

Printed in Singapore

The Colour of Home

Mary Hoffman
Illustrated by Karin Littlewood

FRANCES LINCOLN

"We have a new boy joining us at school today," said Miss Kelly. "He's called Hassan and he's from Somalia. I want you to make him feel at home."

But the classroom didn't feel like home to Hassan at all. In his real home he had lessons out of doors from early in the morning until the sun got too hot at midday. Here he had to stay indoors except in the middle of the day, when he shivered outside in the damp playground.

The children were friendly. They smiled
at Hassan and one of the boys kicked
a football towards him. But he didn't
understand anything that anyone said –
only his name and "hello" and "toilet".
It was tiring remembering even a few
English words.

After lunch, which Hassan didn't eat, because he didn't know what it was, Miss Kelly gave all the children big sheets of gritty grey paper and pinned them to easels. She gave Hassan paintbrushes and a pot of water and showed him where all the colours were. He understood from her smiles and movements that she wanted him to paint a picture, but he had never done such a thing before.

He watched the other children for a while, then chose a bottle of bright blue.

He painted a blue, blue sky, without any clouds. Then a white house, a yellow sun and mimosa trees. Outside the house he made stick figures – himself, his father, his mother holding a bundle that was his baby sister, his grandparents, his uncle, his two cousins. There were nine people outside the house, who all lived inside it.

Then Hassan took more paint and put in the animals – a flock of white sheep, some brown goats and a small sandy creature who was supposed to be his cat.

"What a lovely picture, Hassan," said Miss Kelly. "What beautiful bright colours!"

But Hassan hadn't finished. Now he chose red and orange and painted big flames on the roof of the house. The blue sky changed to a murky purple. He drew another stick figure with a gun, and made black bullets come out of it. He took the red paint again and splattered it on the white walls of the house. He smudged his uncle out of the picture.

"Oh, Hassan," said Miss Kelly. "It's all spoilt. What a shame!"
Hassan didn't know what her words meant, but he heard the
sadness in her voice and knew that she understood his picture.

"What did you do at school today?" asked his mother, when she brought his little sister Naima to collect him.

"Painting," said Hassan.

"Can I see?" she said. All around them, other children were showing their pictures to their mothers.

"No," said Hassan. "The paint is still wet." He didn't want his mother to be sad. "You can see it tomorrow."

The next day, Hassan wanted to tell
Miss Kelly that he must make a new
picture. But she had someone
with her, a Somali lady
wearing a black *hajab* like
his mother's – only she also
wore blue jeans and a black
leather jacket, like a
Western woman.

"Hello, Hassan," said the woman. Then she began to speak to him in Somali. "I'm Fela, I've come to translate for you and help with your English. Miss Kelly thought you might want to tell us about your picture."

So another teacher taught the rest of the class maths, and Hassan sat in the reading corner with Fela and Miss Kelly and his picture.

"That's my house in Somalia," he said, looking at Fela, who put his words into English. "That's my family." And he named them all, right down to the baby. "And that's my cat, Musa, who we had to leave behind."

"And who is this?" asked Miss Kelly, pointing to the smudge near the red splashes.

"That's my uncle Ahmed," said Hassan. And then he told them the whole story — about the noise, the flames, the bullets and the awful smell of burning and blood.

"When the soldiers came, I hid in my
cousins' room," he said. "I didn't find out what
happened to my uncle until later. My father came and fetched
me out from under the bed and said we were leaving.

"We all went straight away, except my uncle. We had no luggage, only my father's prayer mat and *qu'ran*, hidden in Naima's bag of nappies. I wanted to take Musa, my cat, but my mother said we must save ourselves and not the animals. I cried then, not for my uncle, but for Musa.

"We went on a big ship from Mogadishu to Mombasa. Then we lived in a camp for a long time. Naima learned to walk there. It was cold at night and my mother had to queue for our food. People stole things and all my mother's gold jewellery disappeared, but I think that was because we bought tickets to England. My cousins and grandparents stayed behind.

I was frightened when I saw the plane we were going to fly in, because I thought it might have bombs in it. The journey was so long, but I wasn't happy when it was over. Our new country seemed all cold and grey. And the flat we live in is grey too, with brown furniture. We seem to have left all the colours behind in Somalia."

Hassan talked for an hour and then he ran out of words, even in Somali. When he finished, Miss Kelly had tears in her eyes.

"Tell her I want to make another picture," Hassan said to Fela, "for my mother."

Then he played football with the friendly boy, who pointed to himself and said, "Jake".

That afternoon, Hassan painted a new picture. It had blue sky, the white house and the yellow mimosa. But this time there were no people – just sheep and goats and Musa the cat with his long spindly legs. There were no flames or bullets. By going-home time the picture was dry.

"It's beautiful," said
Hassan's mother.
   "It's our home in Somalia,"
said Hassan.
   "I know," said his mother.
"We'll put it on the wall of
our home here in England."
   "Let me push Naima,"
said Hassan, and he walked
home pushing his little sister
in her pushchair.

At home, they showed the picture to his father, who stuck it on the wall. The blue, yellow and white looked bright against the grey paint. Next to it hung the maroon prayer-mat which had come with them on their travels.

And as Hassan looked round the room, he saw other colours – things his mother had made – a green cushion, an orange tablecloth and a pink dress she was sewing for Naima.

Just then the sun came out, and there was blue sky outside their window. Hassan looked at his family and said, "Daddy, can we have a new cat?" and he said "cat" in English. It was one of the new words he had learned today.

Tomorrow he would ask Miss Kelly to tell him the word for "home".

OTHER PICTURE BOOKS IN PAPERBACK FROM FRANCES LINCOLN

AMAZING GRACE
Mary Hoffman
Illustrated by Caroline Binch

Grace loves to act out stories, so when there's the chance to play a part in Peter Pan,
she longs to play Peter. But her classmates say that Peter was a boy, and besides,
he wasn't black... With the support of her mother and grandmother, however, Grace
soon discovers that if you set your mind to it, you can do anything you want.

Chosen as part of the recommended booklist for the National Curriculum Key
Stage 1, English Task 1997, Reading, Level 2
Suitable for National Curriculum English – Reading, Key Stage 1
Scottish Guidelines English Language – Reading, Level B

ISBN 0-7112-0699-6

GRACE AND FAMILY
Mary Hoffman
Illustrated by Caroline Binch

For Grace, family means Ma, Nana and a cat called Paw-Paw, and when Papa invites her
to visit him in The Gambia, she dreams of finding a fairy-tale family straight out of
her story books. But, as Nana reminds her, families are what you make them...

Suitable for National Curriculum English – Reading, Key Stages 1 and 2
Scottish Guidelines English Language – Reading, Levels A and B; Religious and Moral Education – Level B

ISBN 0-7112-0869-7

A TWIST IN THE TAIL
Animal Stories from Around the World
Mary Hoffman
Illustrated by Jan Ormerod

What happens when a sheep makes eyes at a wolf… a fox turns blue …
or a tiny tortoise boasts that he's going to ride into town on an elephant?
Mary Hoffman's ten vibrant retellings bring together a clutch of animal characters
from all over the globe. Jan Ormerod has created sun-splashed illustrations
for this collection that will enchant children everywhere.

Suitable for National Curriculum English – Reading, Levels 1 and 2
Scottish Guidelines English Language – Reading, Levels B and C

ISBN 0-7112-1833-1

Frances Lincoln titles are available from all good bookshops.